Don't frighten the Lion!

By

Margaret Wise Brown

With Pictures by

H. A. Rey

HarperTrophy

A Division of HarperCollinsPublishers

Other HarperCollins Books by Margaret Wise Brown

BIG RED BARN

A CHILD'S GOOD NIGHT BOOK

CHRISTMAS IN THE BARN

THE DEAD BIRD

GOODNIGHT MOON

THE IMPORTANT BOOK

LITTLE CHICKEN

THE LITTLE FIR TREE

THE LITTLE FIREMAN

LITTLE FUR FAMILY

NIBBLE, NIBBLE

THE NOISY BOOK

THE QUIET NOISY BOOK

THE RUNAWAY BUNNY

THE SLEEPY LITTLE LION

SNEAKERS: SEVEN STORIES ABOUT A CAT

TWO LITTLE TRAINS

WAIT TILL THE MOON IS FULL

WHEEL ON THE CHIMNEY

WILLIE'S ADVENTURES

ISBN 0-06-443262-9 (pbk.)
First Harper Trophy edition, 1993.

This book is affectionately dedicated

to

JESSIE STANTON

ONCE there was a little dog who wanted to go to the zoo. She lived near the park, and at night when the wind blew from the park she could hear the seals barking and lion roaring and the monkeys chattering in the monkey house.

So one day her master, who had a mustache, said, "Come on, little dog. I'll take you for a walk in the park and you can see the animals in the zoo."
So they walked through the park.

And they came to the zoo. But there was a big sign that said, NO DOGS allowed in here!

So the little dog and her master had to stop right there. A seal barked and a lion roared and they could hear the monkeys chattering in the monkey house. But they couldn't go in.

They had to turn around and go home.

The little dog was very sad.

Her ears fell down.

And her tail fell down.

And the hair fell down on her back.

She was so sad.

"Look how sad my little dog is," said the little dog's master to the keeper of the zoo. "When we came to the sign that said NO DOGS and we couldn't go in, her ears fell down and her tail fell down and the fur fell down on her back. She is so sad."

The keeper of the zoo was very sorry to see them go, and he said, "If only she were a child or even looked like a child, then she could go in. But a little dog would frighten the animals. Especially the lion!"

"By cracky!" said the little dog's master. "I know what I will do.
I'll dress her up as a child. That's what I'll do. Then she won't
frighten the lion."
So they went to a hairdresser and got the little dog a haircut.

Then they went to a store.
And they bought the little dog
a hat with cherries on it,

And a polka dot dress,
And some striped socks,
And red shoes!

But the little dog still looked something like a little dog.

So they bought her some blue sunglasses,

And a pair of yellow gloves,

And some gladiola perfume.

And the little dog's master taught her to walk on her hind legs.

Then they went to the zoo.

As they walked up to the gate they met the keeper of the zoo.

"How do you do," said the keeper of the zoo.

"What a nice little girl you have there.

"Don't bark, little girl.

Keep off the grass. And don't frighten the lion!"

Then the keeper walked away.

And the little dog, all dressed up like a little girl, went trotting
into the zoo.

Ourhh ourhh ourhh—the seals!

The little dog could see the big slippery seals sliding in and out of the water. And she could smell their cold wet smell. And now she knew what a seal was.

GRRRRRRRRRRRR—A fierce yellow lion! He looked very brave and there was that warm tawny crinkly smell the little dog had smelled so often on the night wind. Now she knew what a lion was. But the lion didn't know who she was.

And they saw a mother panther with a lot of little panthers.

And then they saw the bears. Polar bears,
swimming in cold water and eating fish.

Then they saw brown bears and cinnamon bears.
The bears were eating bread and climbing trees.
The bears smelled like bears.

They saw a raccoon dipping his paws and his food in water,
the way raccoons do.
And they saw the zebras.
The zebras looked like striped horses and they smelled like
horses too, only they barked.

And they saw a red fox

And a kangaroo mother with twins,

And a laughing hyena. Only the laughing hyena didn't laugh.

And then they went into the monkey house.

Nothing but monkeys!!!

There was a baboon eating a banana
And a monkey looking at the world upside down.

There was a little black ape trying to catch
the other little black ape in the mirror.

And some little grey monkeys who were
scratching about in each other's fur.

But just as the little dog
leaned forward to see
what they were scratching for,
one of the monkeys grabbed her hat.
And that wasn't all.
Off went her glasses in the quick fingers of another monkey,
And her gloves,

And her dress and one shoe.

"Woof," said the little dog as her dress flew over her head.

"By cracky," said her master. "You're a dog again.
We had better be going!"

And he took his little dog up in his arms,
tucked her under his coat so that she wouldn't frighten the lion,
and carried her

HOME.